This book belongs to:

Disney's Out & About With Pooh
A Grow and Learn Library

Published by Advance Publishers
© 1996 Disney Enterprises, Inc.
Based on the Pooh stories by A. A. Milne © The Pooh Properties Trust.

Written by Ronald Kidd
Illustrated by Arkadia Illustration Ltd.
Designed by Vickey Bolling
Produced by Bumpy Slide Books

ISBN:1-885222-65-3
10 9 8 7 6 5 4 3 2 1

In the Hundred-Acre Wood there was a bridge. Under the bridge there was a stream, and in the stream there was a boat.

It was a gray boat with floppy ears at one end and a tail at the other. The boat held a flag, and there was a soft, squishy place in the middle where the captain sat.

The captain, whose name was Piglet, said, "It's getting late. I should be going."

"Yes, I suppose you should," sighed Eeyore the boat.

"Don't worry," said Piglet. "I'll be back another time."
Eeyore watched sadly as Piglet hopped ashore and
scampered down the path. Then, dripping wet, Eeyore
trudged off through the forest.

Eeyore lay in bed that night, thinking. No matter how much fun he had during the day, his friends always went home at night, leaving Eeyore alone again. He wished that just once he could have a friend who would stay with him all the time. That's when he thought of a pet.

Eeyore fell asleep dreaming of pets. First he dreamed of a dog. It chased sticks. It sat up. It rolled over. It licked Eeyore's face — a lot.

No matter where Eeyore went, the dog was there, licking his face. In his dream, Eeyore liked having company, but he didn't like being a lollipop.

Next Eeyore dreamed of having a cat. He fed the cat some milk each day. He brushed its fur. He brought out a pillow for the cat to lie on. Before long he was following the cat wherever it went, carrying its milk and brush and pillow.

In his dream, Eeyore decided cats were too much work.

Finally Eeyore dreamed of a parrot. He carried the parrot on his shoulder every day. After a while it started to talk.

"Oh, well," said the parrot.

"What can one expect?" sighed the parrot.

"I suppose that's fine, if you like that sort of thing," said the parrot.

In his dream, Eeyore became so sad listening to what the parrot said that he had to give the bird to Pooh instead.

When Eeyore woke up the next morning, he went for a walk through the forest. As he walked, he pretended that he was speaking to his pet.

Eeyore said, "Fine, thank you. And you?" Then he added, "My, the thistles are lovely this time of year, don't you think?" But his imaginary pet never answered.

After a while Eeyore stopped to rest and noticed a little green lump on a tree branch. While he watched, the lump moved!

The lump turned out to be a caterpillar. The way it moved reminded Eeyore of the way he moved: very, very slowly.

As Eeyore studied the caterpillar, he began to think how it would make the perfect pet. It didn't bark or lick his face. It didn't need a brush or pillow. And it never said anything sad.

Pleased, Eeyore lifted the caterpillar off the branch
and placed it on his back. Then he set out to show Pooh
and Piglet.

He found his two friends on the bridge, playing a game of Poohsticks. In the game, Pooh and his friends would drop sticks off one side of the bridge. Then they would

hurry to the other side and see which stick came out first. Today Pooh thought he was winning the game, but he wasn't sure because all the sticks looked alike.

Eeyore wanted to show Pooh and Piglet his new pet, but he was not the sort of animal who would interrupt a serious game of Poohsticks. Instead he decided to join them.

He played for a bit, then checked to see how his
caterpillar was doing. But when he looked, it was gone!

While Eeyore searched frantically, he heard Pooh say, "Isn't that odd? One of the sticks has a little green lump on it."

Eeyore, fearing the worst, hurried from the bridge and waded into the stream. He floated along next to the stick and looked closely. Sure enough, there was the caterpillar.

Up on the bridge, Piglet called, "Eeyore, what are you doing in the water?"

"Pretending to be a Poohstick?" guessed Pooh.

"No!" Eeyore shouted back. "I'm taking a swim with my new pet!"

Pooh and Piglet pulled Eeyore ashore, and he proudly showed them his caterpillar.

The three friends watched as it crawled along a branch and ate leaves. They counted twelve parts to its body, and three pairs of legs. Both Pooh and Piglet agreed that a caterpillar seemed like a perfect pet indeed. It was quiet, found its own food, and kept Eeyore company wherever he went!

Eeyore spent the next few happy days with his caterpillar. It was with him during the day, when he spent time with his friends.

And, best of all, it was with him at night when his
friends had gone home. Eeyore hoped the caterpillar
would be his pet forever.

When Eeyore woke up the next morning, however, the caterpillar had changed from a soft little green lump into a hard little brown lump. It didn't wiggle or crawl or eat leaves. It just sat there.

So Eeyore sat there, too. He sat there hour after hour, day after day, waiting for the hard brown lump to change back into his perfect pet.

As Eeyore waited, he thought back to the good old days, when he and his caterpillar had romped through the forest without a care in the world.

He grew sadder and sadder, until he was so sad that he knew only his friend Christopher Robin could help.

Eeyore found Christopher Robin and showed him the hard brown lump.

"That lump is a sort of house that caterpillars make to stay inside of when they're changing," the boy explained. "It's called a cocoon."

"Changing?" said Eeyore. "Into what?"

"Into this," Christopher Robin replied. He smiled and pointed to a butterfly, fluttering in the air.

"Oh," Christopher Robin added, "and when the caterpillar is finished changing, it makes a hole in the house and crawls out."

Eeyore looked at the hard brown lump again. There was a hole at one end. Then he gazed up at the butterfly. "Is that my caterpillar?" he asked.

"Yes, it is," said Christopher Robin.

Eeyore tried to catch the butterfly so he could carry it with him, but the butterfly dipped and fluttered away.

Eeyore shook his head sadly and said, "I've lost my
perfect pet, haven't I?"

"Yes," said Christopher Robin, "but look at how
beautiful it is now."

The butterfly spread its wings and rose into the air.
As Eeyore watched, it floated over the flowers and meadows

of the Hundred-Acre Wood. Soon it was joined by other butterflies, brightening the sky.

From then on, whenever Eeyore was lonely, he would think of all those beautiful butterflies, flying out there somewhere, and he wouldn't feel alone anymore.